the FORT that JACK BUILT

by Boni Ashburn

illustrated by Brett Helquist

Abrams Books for Young Readers, New York

The illustrations in this book
were created with oil on a digital print.

Cataloging-in-Publication Data has been applied for
and may be obtained from the Library of Congress.

ISBN: 978-1-4197-0795-7

Text copyright © 2013 Boni Ashburn
Illustrations copyright © 2013 Brett Helquist
Book design by Chad W. Beckerman

Published in 2013 by Abrams Books for Young Readers, an imprint
of ABRAMS. All rights reserved. No portion of this book may be
reproduced, stored in a retrieval system, or transmitted in any form
or by any means, mechanical, electronic, photocopying, recording,
or otherwise, without written permission from the publisher.

Printed and bound in China
10 9 8 7 6 5 4 3 2 1

Abrams Books for Young Readers are available at special discounts
when purchased in quantity for premiums and promotions as
well as fundraising or educational use. Special editions can also
be created to specification. For details, contact specialsales@
abramsbooks.com or the address below.

ABRAMS
THE ART OF BOOKS SINCE 1949
115 West 18th Street
New York, NY 10011
www.abramsbooks.com

03184 5173

For Jack, my little boy with
the big imagination
—B.A.

For Henry and Finn
—B.H.

This is a table.
And two comfy chairs.
A big stack of pillows that came from upstairs.

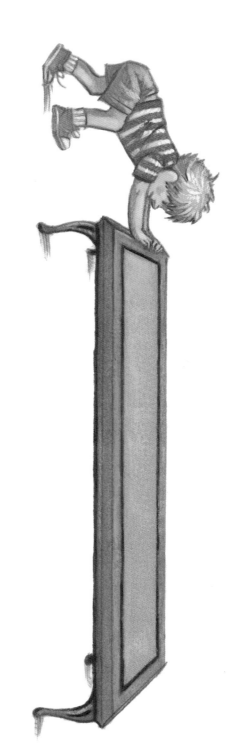

An armload of books.

A breakfast-bar stool.

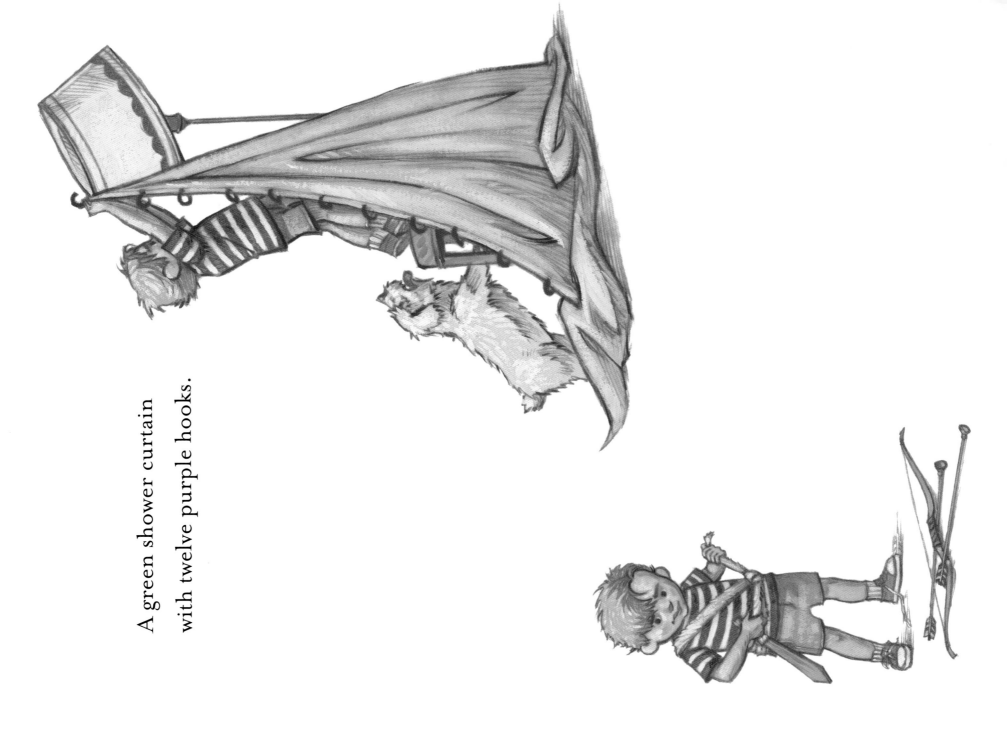

A green shower curtain
with twelve purple hooks.

A dog leash. Striped sheets.
And a huge patchwork quilt.
And . . . .

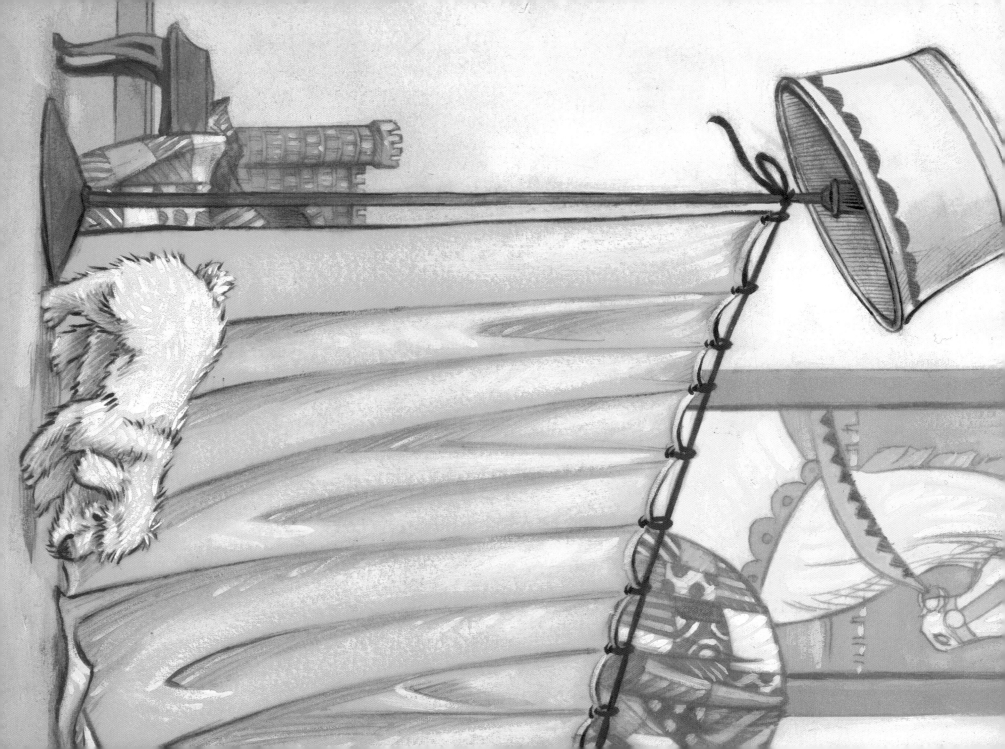

This is the FORT
that JACK BUILT!

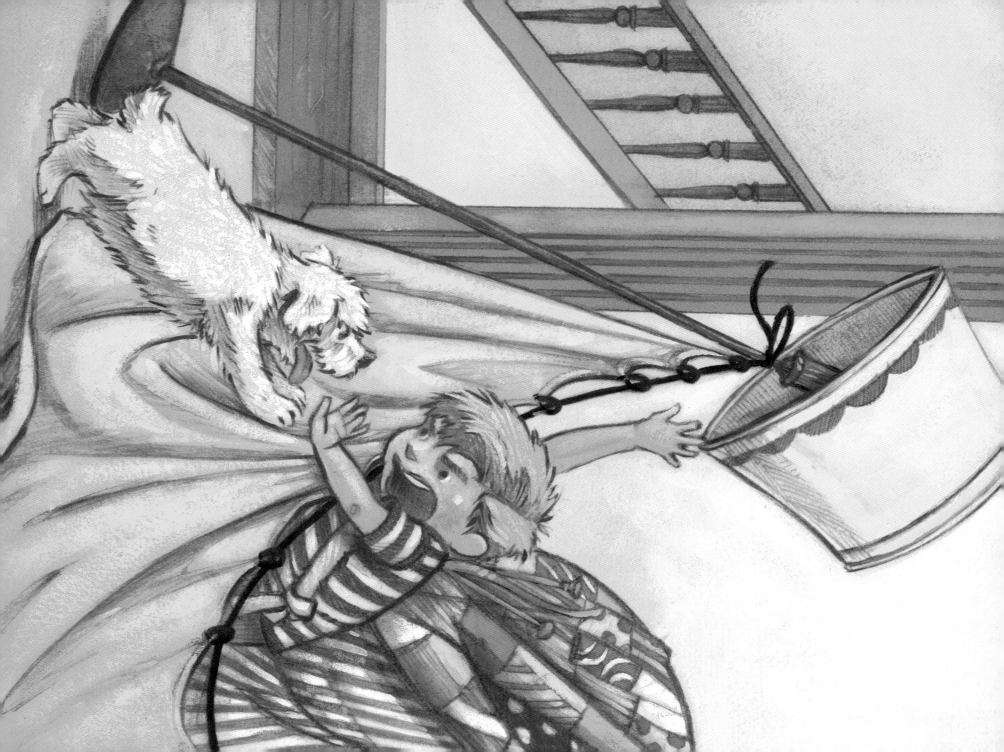

And this is Jack's dog—

"No, Milo!"

WOOF! WAG!

—who almost collapsed the fort that Jack built.

This is Jack's sister—"Hey, who took my chair?"

She yanks it away, creating a sag,

right after the dog *WOOFed!* with a *WAG!*

and almost collapsed the fort that Jack built.

This is Jack's brother—"My books! Give them back!"

He grabs the whole stack, which opens a crack right next to the spot (where the chair was now *not*) by the worsening sag made by Jack's dog, who WOOFed! with a WAG! and almost collapsed the fort that Jack built.

This is Jack's sister (the older one), wet,
wrapped up in a towel—"I wasn't done yet!"
She takes back the curtain with every last hook
(right after Jack's brother took every last book).
So now there's a gap . . . and a crack and a sag
made by Jack's dog, who *WOOFed!* with a *WAG!*
and almost collapsed the fort that Jack built.

This is Jack's mother—"I'm making beds, Jack"—
who needs the striped sheets and the pillow-stack back!
Without sheets or pillows, the curtain, books, chair,
Jack's fort's not the same as it was under there.
New holes, gaps, and cracks,
and way too much sag,
made by Jack's dog, who WOOFed! with a WAG!
and almost collapsed the fort that Jack built.

This is Jack's dad—"I need my chair, Jack!
And your fort . . . I can't see. I can't see the TV!"
There goes the last chair, and the whole northern side,
and the holes and the gaps and the cracks much too wide,
and the sag from the dog,
who WOOFed! with a WAG!
and almost collapsed
the fort that Jack built.

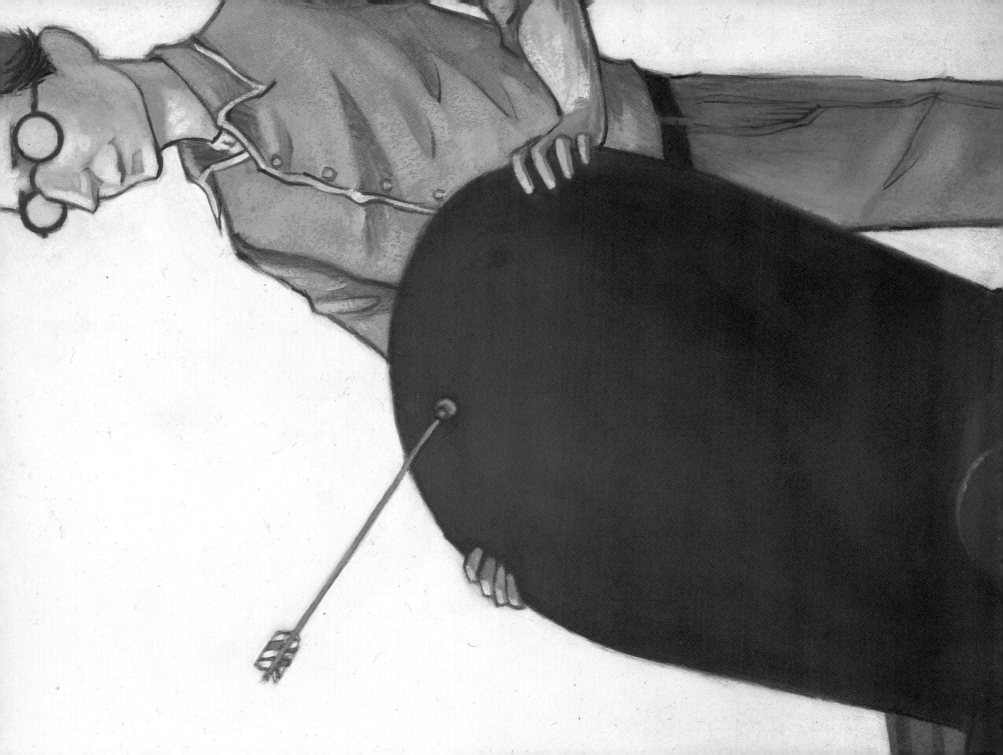

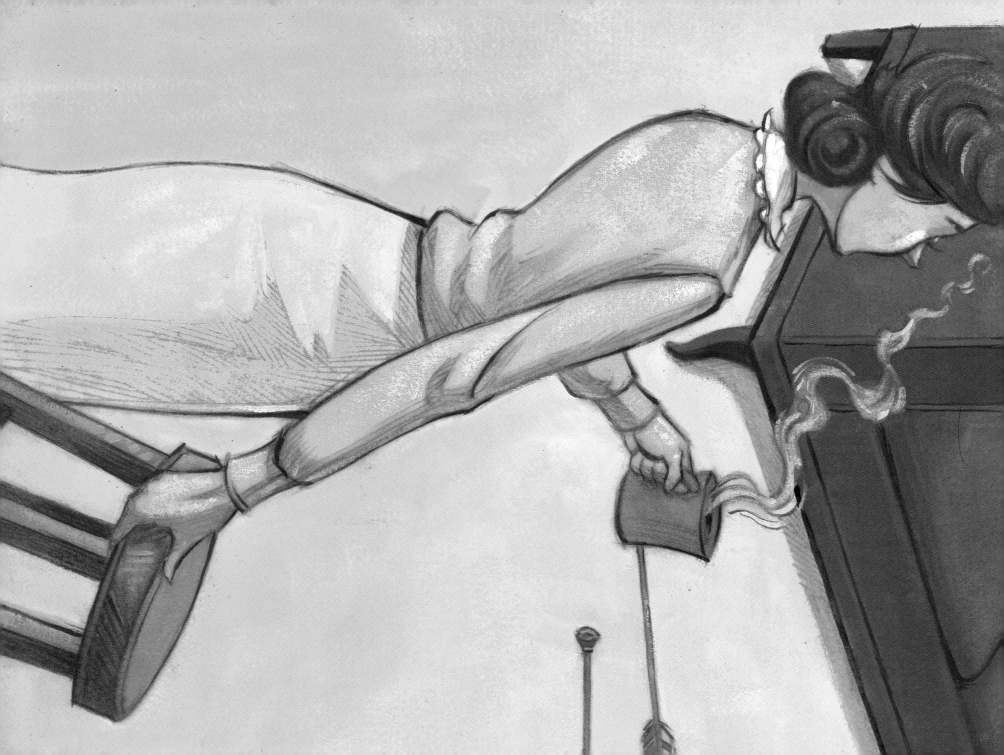

This is Jack's mother—her mug in her hand—
now done with the beds, not willing to stand.
She slips out the stool and says, "See? It's still fine!"

It isn't, thinks Jack, *but at least it's still mine!*

And the cracks are all gone, and so is the sag
made by the dog, who *WOOFed!* with a *WAG!*
and almost collapsed the fort that Jack built.

This is Jack's grandma—"Hey, buddy, what's new?
I think that I'm feeling a bit cold. Are you, too?"
That does it. Poor Jack—he can't take the *guilt*.
He takes down the last of his fort: Grandma's *quilt*.
There are no more cracks, or gaps, or big sags,
no dripping-wet curtains, or dog *WOOFs!* or *WAGs!*
or almost-collapsing of forts made by Jack.

The only thing left is a small coffee table,

and that is the end of our fort-building fable.

Except . . . here's a hint: If you're something like Jack

and you use people's things that they'll likely want back,

they might be more willing (or at least might not care)

if you use all their things but are willing . . .